THE DIM THIN DUCKS

When Kate goes to Chapel Street City Farm with Jenny and Seth to collect some ducks, she has no idea what excitement is to follow. One pair of ducks, Aylesburys, are ordinary enough, but the others, Indian Runners, are most unusual. Nicknamed the dim thin ducks because of their shape and their seeming ignorance of what to do when faced with water, they are the indirect cause of great drama. For, in digging the ducks' pond, Dan and Mike unearth something most unexpected!

Judy Allen is the author of a number of stories for young people and adults, as well as several guide books. Her Walker titles include *Awaiting Developments* (for which she received the Whitbread Children's Novel Award and Friends of the Earth Earthworm Award), *Something Rare and Special* and a second City Farm story, *The Great Pig Sprint*. Two further stories, *The Cheap Sheep Shock* and *The Long-Loan Llama*, are published by Julia MacRae Books.

First published 1990 by
Julia MacRae Books
This edition published 1991 by
Walker Books Ltd, 87 Vauxhall Walk,
London SE11 5HJ

Text © 1990 Judy Allen
Illustrations © 1990 Kate Aldous

Reprinted 1993

Printed and bound in England by Clays Ltd., St. Ives plc.

British Library Cataloguing in Publication Data
A catalogue record for this book is
available from the British Library.
ISBN 0-7445-2009-6

The
Dim Thin Ducks

Judy Allen

Illustrated by
Kate Aldous

WALKER BOOKS
LONDON

Contents

1 The Pony Express

The pony was scared of the train, Kate was scared of the pony, and the donkey didn't like being left alone in the stable.

"This is not a good start," said Kate, clinging to the front of the saddle.

The train was the noisiest of the four of them, clanking across the high viaduct behind the farmyard. As soon as it had gone, though, the other three could be heard clearly – Polka the pony making nervous little neighing noises, Dot the donkey kicking her door, and Kate complaining that she had never wanted to learn to ride anyway.

"Then why did you ask to have a go as soon as you got here today?" said Alison, who was walking by Polka's head, leading her.

"My mother's coming for me this afternoon," said Kate. "I wanted to get this over first."

"Why?"

"She always has her camera. I don't want to know what I look like up here. OH!"

"Now what's the matter?"

"Why's she tossing her head like that? And why are her back feet going sideways?"

Before Alison could answer, there was a splintering crash from behind them as Dot finally succeeded in kicking her stable door off its hinges. Everybody jumped and Polka seemed to change shape under Kate. Her front legs got longer, her back legs got shorter, and her ears swivelled round so that they almost met behind her head.

Kate opened her mouth to tell anyone who was listening that she was not having a nice time, but then closed it again and concentrated on hanging on.

Alison moved quickly in front of Polka and tried to soothe her.

People in various parts of the farm dropped whatever they were doing and ran towards the stables.

Before anyone could get there, however, Dot walked calmly out, clomping noisily over the door, which now lay on the ground, and then trotted briskly along the beaten earth track until she reached Polka. Looking down, Kate saw the small grey figure come up beside the pony and stop level with her. As soon as Dot was next to her, Polka went back to being a normal shape again. Her back feet stopped walking sideways, her ears straightened out and the noises she was making began to sound cheerful instead of anxious. Alison loosened her hold on the bridle so that the two could greet each other properly.

Dan, Seth and Jenny ran up beside the donkey, but didn't try to catch her.

"It was my fault, Alison," said Jenny breathlessly, dragging her hair back more firmly through its rubber band. "I shouldn't have told you to leave Dot behind. They're obviously not ready to be parted yet, not even by such a short distance."

"Homesick, I suppose," said Alison, still holding Polka's bridle with one hand but using the other to stroke each head in turn. "It IS only two weeks since they got here."

"It was the train that did it," said Kate, still holding on tightly but feeling safe enough to speak now. "She was frightened of the Pony Express!"

She thought that was a very witty remark, but not for long.

"Express!" said Dan. "That was a local passenger train!"

"She knows as much about trains as she does about animals," said Seth.

"Oh belt up," said Alison. "The train DID upset her — what does it matter what sort it was?"

"I think I'd like to get down now," said Kate.

"She mustn't, must she?" said Dan, looking at Jenny. At fifteen, he thought he knew most things without asking, but he could just about bear to admit that Jenny had worked with animals for more years than he'd lived.

"No, she must do the full circuit," said Jenny firmly. "Otherwise she could lose her nerve."

"I've already lost it," said Kate pathetically.

"Not you," said Jenny, "Polka. Don't look like that, Kate, you're doing fine."

Seth grinned.

"Come on," said Alison, leading the pony forward

again. "She'll be all right now she's got Dot with her."

Kate was quite sure that if she let herself burst into tears someone would help her out of the uncomfortably swaying saddle that seemed such a long way above the stony ground. She was also quite sure that she mustn't so much as whimper in front of Dan, who thought she was too young to belong to the Junior Farmers' Club in the first place, or in front of Seth, who agreed with him. So she looked straight ahead, patted the top of the farm's second-best hard hat, to reassure herself it was still on her head, and kept quiet.

Alison led Polka on along the track that went around the outside of Lee Road Farm, just inside the fence. The little grey donkey kept pace with them, her head nodding as she walked. The pony's head nodded, too, at exactly the same rhythm.

Unlike Polka, Dot wasn't disturbed by all the new things around her. She noticed the trains all right, and she was interested in the goats, geese, pigs, hens and visiting children, none of which either of them had been used to in their former country-house home, but she didn't fuss – she just studied them

calmly and decided they weren't dangerous. The
single thing she couldn't bear was being separated
from Polka.

There was something altogether reassuring about
Dot, and Kate was beginning to see why Polka
became quiet as soon as she was near.

"I like having Dot with us," she said.

"So do I," said Alison. "I won't try to stop her
again."

They passed behind the large goose-pen and
Gander stretched up tall and flapped his wings at
them in case they were planning an attack on either
of his wives. As well as the fence around the outside

of his pen, there was a new small fence across the middle. There were to be ducks, very soon, and no one was quite sure how Gander would feel about that.

Kate looked across the goose-pen at the main farmyard, sheltered at the back by the brick-built office and dairy, the goat-houses and, after a gap, the pig-sties. The hens were scratting about in a vague sort of way and, as usual, one was riding comfortably on the back of a sheep.

"Now the sheep are shorn," said Kate, "I should think the hens' claws would hurt."

"They're thick-skinned," said Alison.

The goats were all in their big pen, though Mike had promised they could have a bit more freedom when the vegetable patches were securely fenced. ("They could eat six months' work in ten minutes," he said, "if they all got down to it together.") The three goat kids were resting in a heap; the three nanny goats were standing about looking wise, and Kate waved at Cleopatra, her favourite, who gazed across the farmyard at her.

"She must think I'm mad, sitting up here like this," said Kate, as they passed out of Cleopatra's sight behind the buildings.

"I doubt it," said Alison. "I'm sure you're the only one here who thinks riding a pony is a weird thing to do."

They followed the track around, passing on their right the big area behind the buildings where there was nothing yet but the small vegetable patch, in the middle, and the curved polythene shape of the makeshift greenhouse. To their left loomed the huge dark arch of the dirty brick railway viaduct. The far side of it was boarded up so that the space underneath was more like a cave than a tunnel. Polka pulled her head up a bit as they passed, and rolled her eyes rather, but Dot refused to be spooked and she settled again.

"I'm with Polka," said Kate. "I think it's creepy, too."

"There are plans to build workshops under there eventually," said Alison, "for a saddlemaker and a spinner and a weaver."

"I expect there are spinners there already," said Kate. "Spidery spinners."

The track curved full circle, leading to the row of new stables, beyond the pig-sties. The original plan had been to build just one double stable for Polka and Dot, who had been given to the farm as a present. But once work started, it just seemed to keep going, and one day when Kate arrived to milk

Cleopatra she saw there was a row of six. ("No idea who's going to live in the others," said Jenny. "We'll just have to hope something turns up.")

Kate got down from Polka, with Alison's help. Once on the ground she stood very still, afraid that if she tried to walk her legs might set off in opposite directions.

"It was so much better having Dot with us," said Alison to Jenny, who was waiting for them. "She's a good influence."

"She's very sensible, isn't she?" said Jenny, rubbing the donkey's grey nose.

"That is NOT how I'd describe her," said George bitterly, propping the damaged stable door against the doorpost. "I'll have to rehang this − fit the hinges to the other side. She's done too much damage for me to put 'em back where they were."

"All in a good cause, wasn't it Dot?" said Alison.

"Feel free to sympathise with me if you want to," said George.

"Oh, you love fixing things," said Jenny, "you know you do."

"I like building things," said George, picking a splinter out of his thumb. "It isn't the same."

"Mike'll help you," said Jenny. "I can't – I've got to take Amelia over to Chapel Street Farm and bring the ducks back. Anyone like to come for the ride? Kate?"

"If you mean a ride in a car and not a ride on a horse," said Kate, "I would like to. Thank you."

2 Four Ducks for a Pig

Dan waded into the pig-sty among Abel, Amy, Arnold, Alban, Aylmer, Ada and Adeline and separated out Amelia, who was quite happy to be shepherded into the farmyard. Jenny, meanwhile, had reversed her big battered car in through the farm gate, which Mike and Seth opened for her and then closed behind her.

Dan held a plastic bowl of pigswill about five inches from Amelia's snout, and she followed it across the farmyard and up the plank onto the newspapers in the luggage space of the car. Dan set the bowl down on the floor. Amelia sank her face gratefully into it, and didn't even glance up when the door was slammed down behind her.

"Do you two mind sitting in the back, in case she gets upset?" said Jenny.

Kate, who had thought she and Amelia were to be the only passengers, glanced round, wondering who else was coming. She wasn't especially pleased to see that it was Seth, who usually treated her as if she was an exceptionally stupid three-year-old. But she got in anyway.

The regular policeman, P.C. Frazer, was strolling down the road as they pulled out of the farm gate. Although the road was clear, he pretended to hold up the traffic for them, smiling broadly.

"I bet we make his beat more interesting," said Kate.

At first Seth ignored Kate completely. He sat
twisted round on the back seat, talking to the pig
through the mesh screen that stopped her jumping
forward into the car. Amelia, who had sat down
suddenly when the car began to move, got to her feet
again and stood as still as she could for about half a
mile, swaying gracefully as they turned corners.
Then she caught sight of the passing view and began
to totter first to one side window, then back to the
other, to and fro, to and fro, the newspapers rustling
fussily under her feet.

"Is she all right?" said Jenny, keeping her eyes on
the road.

"Dunno," said Seth. "She's excited, but I'm not
sure if it's happy-excited or cross-excited."

"As long as she's not frightened," said Jenny.

"Don't think so," said Seth. "I think she's
jogging."

"She was the best sprinter," said Kate, "when we
had the pig races. Perhaps she's keeping in practice."

"She's wearing me out, that's what," said Seth.

Jenny caught Kate's eye in the rear-view mirror.
"How did you get on with Polka?" she said.

"All right," said Kate. "I'm glad I tried it. But I

don't think I'll ever be a rider."

"Or a farmer," said Seth automatically.

"I might be a farmer," said Kate. "I'm good with goats."

"If you mean Cleopatra," said Seth, "she likes everyone."

"No, be fair," said Jenny, pulling up at a set of traffic lights. "It's true she's even-tempered, but she is especially fond of Kate. Took to her the minute she saw her, Mike says."

A van pulled up beside them at the lights, and then forgot to move on when they changed to green.

"Did you see his face?" said Jenny, as she drove away, leaving the van standing. "He thought he saw a pig in the back of our car!"

"Anyway," said Seth, unwilling to stop needling Kate, "farmers are men."

"I'm not," said Jenny.

"MOST farmers are men," said Seth.

Jenny didn't seem to have an answer to that. Amelia began to make cheerful grunting sounds to the same beat as her trotting feet.

"The all-singing, all-dancing pig!" said Seth.

Kate thought for a bit and then said, "Most farmers may be men, but most farm animals are women."

"What about bulls and rams and billy goats," said Seth at once.

"But there's only ever one bull and lots of cows," said Kate. "And we haven't got a ram or a billy goat at all."

"We take the nannies to the billy," said Seth. "The ram came to us last time. You must know there's got to be a male if you want any more of anything."

"Only *one* male," said Kate. "All our goats are women, even the kids, all the hens are women, except the cockerel, the pony and the donkey are women, there are two women geese and one Gander . . ."

"You know she's right, Seth," said Jenny. "Farmers usually prefer to see females born than males. Most male goat kids, for example, are sold for meat or put to sleep soon after birth."

"Oh," said Kate, wishing she hadn't begun this conversation.

Seth was quiet for a bit, too, and then he said, "If this pig-jog goes on, she'll have walked the whole way there."

Kate had a worrying thought. "Why are we taking her?" she said. "What are they going to do with her?"

"Breed from her," said Jenny, "as soon as she's old enough. And give us two pairs of ducks in exchange."

Kate was just about to ask what would happen to the rest of the litter, when Seth said, "Is this it?" and Jenny said, "This is it," at the same time.

"I'll park here for a moment," said Jenny, drawing up at the roadside, "and go and ask if they want me to drive in, or if someone's going to come and carry her. Will you two wait with her?" She got out of the car while she was speaking, and slammed the door, not leaving Kate and Seth much choice.

Amelia stopped when the car stopped, and stood still for a moment, looking around with her small, inquisitive eyes. But the door-slam was too much for her, after everything else, and the inevitable happened.

"Look what she's done!" said Kate. "Oh, phoooo!"

"It's that Dan, feeding her," said Seth, winding down the window beside him. "Open your one."

"I don't think it helps much," said Kate, sticking her head right out of the window on the pavement side. "Hey – Chapel Street Farm looks a lot bigger than ours."

Amelia trotted daintily away from the cause of all the trouble, as though it had nothing to do with her, and stood on the other side of the luggage space, behind Kate, staring at the outer fences of the farm.

"She thinks it's bigger, too," said Kate. "Look at her face. She's impressed."

"I can't stand this," said Seth. "I'll have to get out."

"We aren't supposed to."

"I'm not GOING anywhere," said Seth, opening the door. "I just want to breathe."

They stood side by side, leaning against the car, careful not to block Amelia's view.

"It's got more buildings than we've got," said Kate.

"We're new," said Seth. "This is old. That's all."

Jenny reappeared, with two men who opened the double gates and pointed to a bit of tarmac by the main building where she could park.

"I wouldn't get in if I was you," said Seth. "I'd push it."

"Oh she hasn't, has she?" said Jenny. "Lucky it didn't happen sooner, I suppose."

Amelia's new sty was quite near the tiny car park, and Seth and Jenny guided her in without much trouble. Once inside, she pottered about, quite unworried, inspecting the house and run.

"I'll get the ducks," said one of the two men, strolling off. "They're all crated up."

"I'll help you muck out the car," said the other one. He nodded at Seth and Kate. "Why don't you two go and have a look around?"

"Sure," said Seth, and strode off at once. Kate, who was a bit overwhelmed by the place, hurried along just behind him. She preferred to keep someone familiar in view, even if it was only sarcastic Seth.

Chapel Street Farm seemed enormous. It, too, was beside a railway line – part of the same line that passed Lee Road Farm, Kate found out later – but it was much longer and wider. There were ten stables in a row, though without any horses in them. There were four pig-sties, all of them fully occupied. ("Why do they need Amelia?" said Kate.) There was a great line of goat-houses, with fenced runs in front of them and pretty white goats inside. There were several hen coops, two proper brick-built houses for the ducks and geese, a shelf-full of hutches under a sloping roof, each with an angora rabbit crouched inside, and an exceedingly big pen with several different kinds of sheep in it. There was even a small black cow.

Then, when they'd passed all this, they came on a huge exercise area for the horses. They could see now why the stables had been empty. A line of horses, each with a young rider on its back, was walking around the arena, obeying the instructions of a girl in the centre. Beyond the arena they could see an allotment, full of flowers and vegetables and with apple trees at the edges.

It goes on forever, Kate thought.

A boy was leaning on the fence, watching the horses, and he turned his head as they came up. "Hi," he said to Seth, not seeming to notice Kate at all. "You're from Lee Road, aren't you?"

"Yup."

"We came to your Open Day last month. Thought I recognised you. You're the one who let the kid escape, aren't you?"

"Not me," said Seth, glaring.

"He was the one who caught it," said Kate, wanting things to be fair.

The boy turned right around and stood up straight. He was bigger than Seth, about Dan's height. He leant his back against the fence, put his hands in his jeans pockets, and said, "Not much to see at your farm, is there?"

"Enough," said Seth, and he turned away to walk back to the car.

"You haven't even got stables," said the boy. He had a sneer on his face that made Dan's worst expression seem positively kindly.

Seth stopped. "That's all you know," he said. "We've got six stables."

"Yeah?" said the boy. "Well we've got TEN horses. From what I hear, you've got one clapped out old pony and a donkey."

Seth opened his mouth to say something. Nothing came out.

So Kate shouted. She shouted because the boy was

pretending she didn't exist and she felt she had to shout to get his attention. "But when you wanted a really good pig," (she shouted), "you had to ask us, didn't you?" And she turned and ran before he could come up with anything else.

She and Seth reached the gate together, and Jenny said, "Oh good, I was just going to call you. Get in."

In the luggage compartment behind the mesh two small crates quacked softly to themselves, and eight eyes glittered through the wide-apart slats.

"Silly nerd!" said Seth.

"Stupid twit!" said Kate.

"Thinks he knows it all," said Seth.

"WE told him!" said Kate.

"Yeah, we told him," said Seth.

3 The Dim Thin Ducks

As the car turned in at Lee Road Farm, Kate said sadly, "Chapel Street's got a LOT more animals, hasn't it?"

"We'll catch up," said Jenny.

"We'll be better," said Seth.

"We'll show them!" said Kate, cheering up.

"We'll have llamas, and all sorts," said Seth.

"We'll see," said Jenny.

Kate got out of the car. The farm seemed especially quiet that day. It was summer-holiday-time and there were no visiting school parties. Even some of the regular Junior Farmers were away or off on days out somewhere. Mike and George were still there, though, rehanging the mended stable door.

Alison was nearby, grooming Polka while Dot looked on. Supervising, Kate thought. Dan was stooping about in the second pig-sty, mucking out the young ones.

Kate went over to tell Abigail that Amelia seemed to like her new home. The big sow, who was rootling in some straw in the corner of her yard, came over to the sty wall at once, always glad of company, and peered at Kate with her narrow, smiley eyes.

"Your daughter's gone up in the world," said Kate. "Though she wasn't on her best behaviour during the trip."

Abigail snorted.

"That's what *I* thought," said Kate.

She went over to the goats and scratched Cleopatra's ears, at the top where they joined her head. "Chapel Street Farm may be posh," she said, "but they haven't got any like you, so we're more special."

Talking to Cleopatra reminded her of the story about the male goat kids, the one she would rather have forgotten; and that in turn reminded her of the question she hadn't asked Seth. She left the goats and walked rather reluctantly over to Dan.

"What happens to these pigs?" she said.

Dan straightened up. "We may keep Amy," he said, "and breed from her. The rest will go next week. Pork and bacon."

Kate put her hand over her mouth.

"This isn't Pets' Corner," said Dan. "This is a farm and we breed pigs for meat. You're not going to be a baby, are you?"

Kate shook her head vigorously, then turned and began to walk away, towards the spare half of the goose pen, where the ducks had just been let out.

"Hey!" came Dan's voice from behind her.

Kate stopped.

"Did you know Abigail's pregnant again?" said Dan, quite kindly.

"Oh," said Kate.

"She was mated as soon as the As were weaned," said Dan, "just before you came. In a couple of months you may see the B-team being born."

Kate nodded. And then plodded across the farmyard to look at the new ducks.

One pair of ducks was all right. They were white with yellow beaks and they were duck-shaped.

"Aylesburys," Jenny said.

The other pair was white with yellow beaks, too, but they weren't duck-shaped at all, they were tall and narrow, like skittles. For an awful moment Kate thought someone must have pulled them out through the slats of their crate and stretched them.

"Are they all right?" she said.

"They're weird," said Seth.

"They're Indian Runners," said Jenny, heaving the crates out of the pen. "They lay well. We should get plenty of eggs once they settle."

Alison wandered up to have a look. "What tall thin ducks," she said. "And why do they look so surprised?"

"They need to adjust to their new surroundings," said Jenny.

George had built a neat wooden duck-house to match the goose-house on the other side of the dividing fence. None of the ducks went anywhere near it, though, they just paddled about slowly and uncertainly on the scrubby ground, quacking softly to themselves.

Beyond the partition, Gander and his two wives watched but didn't threaten.

"Aren't they quiet?" said Kate. "Compared with hens. They sound as if they've swallowed their voices."

"Don't ducks have to have a duck pond?" said Seth.

"They do fine without," said Jenny, "as long as they can get their heads wet. I must get them a bowl of water." She turned round and then caught sight of something. "Oh look," she said, "I'd forgotten we had that."

Mike and George were staggering across the farmyard towards them, walking with short fast steps, their outside arms held out straight, carrying a metal container between them.

"The old zinc bath," said Jenny. "We found it in a thicket of weeds when we were clearing the space for the vegetable beds. It'll be ideal."

Mike and George heaved the bath over into the pen, slopping water on to the ground. The ducks scattered, muttering anxiously in the backs of their throats. The Aylesburys went in opposite directions, but the tall thin ducks stayed close together.

"You should have brought it empty," said Jenny, "and filled it here. I think the hose would reach."

"NOW she tells us," said George.

"I wanted them to have it quickly," said Mike. "They look a bit distraught."

Dan came over, his gumboots showing signs of having been in the pig-pen. He was carrying a length of slatted wood which he handed to Jenny. She propped it against the side of the bath, as a ramp, and then stepped out of the enclosure.

"Let's stand well back while they settle in," she said. "Kate – here's your mother."

Kate looked round to see her mother crossing the farmyard, her camera, in its case, over her shoulder. "New arrivals?" she said, as she reached them.

"It's all right," said Kate. "Those two are meant to look like that."

"Would you like a photo of them?" said her

mother to Jenny.

"Great!" said Jenny. "It'll be nice to have a record of our early days."

Kate's mother crouched at the edge of the enclosure to take pictures at duck-height.

The two Aylesburys seemed quite content. They had become used to people at Chapel Street, and perhaps were glad to find themselves in a space with fewer other ducks. It was hard to be sure, though, how the Indian Runners felt. They didn't hide, or flap, but they did keep extremely close together, walking quickly about, shoulder to shoulder, looking as though they would be holding hands if they had any. They kept well clear of the tin bath.

"Those two don't look very relaxed, do they?" said Mike, scratching his beard, the way he did when he was worried.

"Difficult to look relaxed," said George, "if you're designed so you stand to attention all the time."

The Aylesburys advanced on the tin bath as soon as it appeared, and walked round it several times, aiming an occasional blow at it with their yellow beaks. On the first few circuits they walked under the ramp. Then one of them waddled up it to the top, quacked at the water, and launched itself in. It had a brief swim, plunged its head under a few times, then got out and went to inspect a patch of weeds by the fence in case it concealed a tasty snack.

The second Aylesbury, which had followed it into the water, stayed longer, ducking its head, flicking its wings and showering so many drops over the edge that the thin ducks began to look interested. They shuffled closer. They were tall enough to see the water quite easily, but because of their upright shape they looked as if they were standing on tiptoe.

"Why don't they get in?" said Dan. "You can see they want to."

"I think they're waiting till the other duck's finished," said Kate. "They look sort of polite."

Then one of the thin ducks approached the ramp from the side and made a vague flapping movement with its foot, as if it thought it might be able to get up that way.

"I don't think they know how," said Jenny.

"The thin ducks are dim ducks," said Seth.

By now the Aylesbury was showing off. It swam in tight circles. It dived under the surface. It reared up so that it seemed to walk on the water, and then it beat its wings as though trying to see how high it could splash.

The dim thin ducks gave up trying to solve the mystery of the ramp and stood together at the end of the bath furthest from the Aylesbury's water-dance. They rested their chins on the edge, like two white umbrellas hooked onto the rim by their handles, and stared.

Most of the watchers laughed, except George, who shook his head in disbelief, and Mike, who said, "I can't stand this — they're breaking my heart."

"Can't we lift them up and put them in?" said Kate, who felt a bit guilty for laughing.

"No," said Jenny. "It's best not to interfere too much."

"We could dig a hole and sink the bath to the rim," said George, "so they could just step in."

Mike looked at Jenny. He was scratching his beard with both hands at once by now. "I think we should?" he said, making it sound like a question.

"*I* think we should," Jenny agreed.

"I'll get a spade," said Dan.

"I came to fetch you home," said Kate's mother, to Kate, "but we could stay and watch for a few minutes if you like."

In fact, they stayed so long that Kate's father got home from work early to an empty house and, guessing where they were, walked over to the farm to find them.

"You're going to take forever at this rate," Jenny was saying as he arrived.

Dan was standing at one end of a hole, which wasn't deep enough yet, leaning on a spade. Mike was standing at the other end, leaning on another spade. The ducks were all standing well back, near their house. George, and Kate's mother, were examining things the digging had turned up.

"This is pretty," said Kate's mother, holding out a piece of broken china. "Willow pattern – you can just see the picture of the little bridge."

Dan shifted two more spadesful of earth.

"Look," said George, reaching down to pick up a little brown bottle. "Medicine bottle – undamaged."

Jenny made a face at Kate's father. "It's been like this for the past half-hour," she said. "They're only trying to sink that bath – not dig the foundations for a skyscraper."

Mike dug a bit more, then stopped and stared.

"Oh, do get on with it," said Jenny.

"But I've hit something hard," said Mike.

"So've I," said Dan, leaning on his spade again.

"NOW what?" said Jenny.

"Alien spaceship," said Seth.

"Unexploded bomb," said Kate's father.

"Buried treasure," said Kate.

"Underground pipe," said George.

"Yes," said Mike, "probably a pipe. We'll have to start again, further over."

"No," said Dan, scratching with his spade. "It ends here, look. We can dig it out."

Mike began to scrape a shallow trench, away from Dan. "It's long," he said.

"I think perhaps you should be careful," said Kate's father.

"Oh YOU," said Kate's mother, going over to him and giving him a hug. "You always have to worry, don't you?"

"I've found the other end," said Mike. "Here it is. The whole thing must be about five foot long. Too much hard work to get it out, let's cover it over and start again."

"Too much hard work to start again," said Dan.

"You may as well dig it free and heave it out," said George. "The hole'll be too long for the bath, but you can pack the spare earth around it."

"I don't want to be annoying," said Kate's father, raising his voice a little to get their attention, "but I wonder if we should get advice. This WAS a bomb site in the war, didn't someone say?"

Everyone looked at him in silence. Mike and Dan stepped out of the hole. Then everyone looked at the rusty metal cylinder they'd partly uncovered.

Jenny said, "I wonder if we should move the ducks."

George said, "Probably only an old boiler from the railway."

Kate said, "Could we ask our policeman?"

Mike said, "Maybe we SHOULD ring the police."

"No," said Kate, "I mean, he's walking past."

He came when they called him, not hurrying, smiling, saying as he got closer, "Got some new ducks for me to meet, have you?"

Then he looked in the hole.

"Oh," he said, and his hand went up to his radio. "Well, I think we'll get someone out to look at this, sharpish. In the meantime I'd leave it strictly alone if I were you."

4 The Unexpected Pond

"I can't go home for tea in the middle of an unexpected bomb," said Kate.

Dan gave a shout of laughter. "UNEXPLODED bomb, you twit," he said.

"Oh leave her alone," said Seth. "It's unexploded AND unexpected."

"Oho!" said Dan. "One car ride together and now this. She's a bit young for you, isn't she?"

Seth made a face at him and walked away.

Kate scowled.

Her mother had walked on ahead to take a picture of Polka and Dot looking out over their stable door, but her father heard.

"Does Dan tease you?" he said.

Kate shrugged and made a noise that sounded like "Pffff", which was a short way of saying that he did, quite a lot, but that she didn't care, or at least didn't care much, or anyway didn't want anyone to know that she cared.

"Would you like me to have a word with him?" said her father.

Kate said, "NO," which was a loud way of saying that she definitely would not like that at all.

"I do understand why you want to stay and watch," said her father, changing the subject rapidly. "I'd like to myself. Let's go home and have tea now and then we can come down again afterwards."

"Oh," said Kate, brightening. "Right."

By the time they'd eaten tea, washed up and walked the three roads back to the farm, quite a lot seemed to have happened.

A large white landrover with a blue light flashing on the top was parked outside. Behind it stood two police cars. Inside the farm, near the duck and goose enclosure, they could see a great many people. P.C. Frazer was still there, and so were several other police officers, plus two soldiers, not to mention Dan, Seth, Alison, George, Mike and Jenny.

"Bomb Disposal Crew's here," said Kate's father, reading the lettering on the side of the landrover. "They're taking it seriously!"

"You must have been right," said her mother. "I'm sorry I laughed at you."

Kate's father smiled. Then he frowned. "I'd rather have been wrong," he said.

Kate led the way in through the farm gate and round to where they all stood. A policewoman walked to meet them, shaking her head. "I'm afraid the farm's closed to visitors," she said.

"I'm not visitors," said Kate. "I'm a Junior Farmer."

The policewoman smiled. "All the same," she said, "we're going to have to move everyone out – junior farmers, senior farmers, animals and all."

Jenny came up behind her saying, "Most of our volunteers are on holiday. We may need the help of these people."

"Anything we can do, of course," said Kate's mother.

The policewoman nodded and stood aside to let them join the group.

Dan grabbed Kate's arm. "Captain Welsh, the BDO, says it IS a UXB," he said, and his eyes glittered a challenge.

Kate stared up at him for a long, silent moment. Then, "That means the Bomb Disposal Officer says it IS an Unexploded Bomb," she said.

Dan looked disappointed and then, surprisingly, he grinned. "Just testing," he said.

"Is this a good place to stand, in that case?" said Kate's father, his eyebrows at an anxious angle.

Captain Welsh looked very relaxed. "If it hasn't done anything in forty-odd years," he said, "it's not going to do anything in the next few hours. But we must immunise it, so we're going to have to clear the immediate area."

"I don't see how we can," said Jenny desperately. "We have five sheep, six goats, eight pigs, assorted poultry, one pony and a donkey."

"It won't be for long," said Captain Welsh. "Twenty-four hours at most — maybe much less."

"But where will they all go?" said Jenny.

"How long have we got?" said Mike.

"As long as it takes," said Captain Welsh. "I won't start until all livestock are clear."

"It would be appreciated if you'd get a move on, though," said the most senior-looking policeman. "The trains have been stopped. Passengers are being bussed between stations. Captain Welsh's back-up crew are on their way. We're already evacuating the flats over there." He nodded his head at the block on the other side of the road. "That won't take long, especially as the shops are shut for the night."

"And luckily," said P.C. Frazer, "most of that block's due for refurbishment anyway."

"You mean it's going to get blown up?" said Seth, startled.

"No!" said the policeman. "I mean very few of the flats are still occupied. Not too many people to move out."

"How big is the bomb?" said Dan. He tried to sound laid-back about it, but Kate could see he was excited.

"Two hundred and fifty kilograms," said the Captain. "We'll need a clearance of about five hundred metres."

Jenny looked wildly around the farm. "I wonder if we shouldn't let the animals take their chance," she said to Captain Welsh. "After all, you are."

"Not Cleopatra!" said Kate. "Not the Dim Thin Ducks!"

"Not any of them," said Captain Welsh. "Worrying about them is the last thing I need. It'll make me nervous if they're here."

"I don't think you have any idea how difficult it's going to be to move a pregnant sow," said Jenny.

"I'm sure you'll manage," said Captain Welsh

cheerfully. "You don't want to see the pig jump over the moon, do you?"

"We've got a yard," said Kate eagerly. "We could have Cleopatra." She imagined herself telling them all at school next term, 'I had a friend to stay in the holidays. She's a goat, actually ...'

"Oh," said her mother. "I don't know ..."

"The only way to our back yard is through the house," said Kate's father. "I don't think ..."

"No!" said Mike.

"Impossible!" said Jenny.

Kate sighed. She had thought the idea was too nice to come true. Much later, though, her mother pointed out that it was her offer to have Cleopatra that somehow got things moving. People began to make telephone calls and plans of action, and the evacuation of Lee Road Farm began in earnest.

The police said they would find space for Polka and Dot at the police-horse stables, which were not far away. When the police horse-box arrived, the driver brought news that another stable had been cleared for the six goats.

"Cleopatra'll think she's been arrested," wailed Kate.

"Polka'll freak out," said Dan.

"Cleopatra will be fine," said Jenny firmly, "and Dot will look after Polka." She did agree, though, that Alison should go too, to settle them all in for the night.

(The police promised to take Alison safely home afterwards. "Thanks," she said, "but you can drop me round the corner. I don't want the neighbours to get the wrong idea.")

Chapel Street Farm had agreed to take as many animals as they could, and to drive over straight away to make the first collection.

("They've got a proper van for transporting animals," said Mike. "They would have," said Seth.)

The horse-box drove off, with a lot of bleating and whinnying going on inside, and almost at once the big Chapel Street van reversed in at the gates.

"You need a sheep-dog," said Kate's father as the small flock showed signs of scattering. Fortunately, though, he and George managed to get Eunice, the biggest and oldest ewe, up the ramp and inside, ignoring her loud complaints. Once she was in the others followed, helped by a few shoves from the rear.

"I don't want the ducks to go back to Chapel Street so soon," said Jenny. "It'll unsettle them. We'll crate them up again and Mike and I can have them in our back yard. Gander and his wives, too. They're used to being shut up at night, they may not mind too much. It'll mean two trips with my car, though."

"No problem," said the senior policeman. "We'll rustle up the dog handlers' van, minus dogs, and do it in one."

"If we couldn't have the goats," said Kate, without much hope, "we're not going to be able to have the pigs, are we?"

"Chapel Street gets the pigs on the next trip," said Jenny, "but ... I don't suppose ..." She looked from Kate's mother to her father and back again. "It's a lot to ask, but the sooner we're clear, the sooner they can defuse the thing, and the sooner we can get all the animals back. I just wondered ... as you live quite near ..."

And that was how Kate's parents ended up with two long, narrow hen houses in their back yard, delivered in a police van and carried through the house by four breathless policemen.

"Hens!" said Kate in disgust, picking up a stray feather from the hall carpet. "Hens are the things I like least, and that's what we get."

"I don't suppose they'll make that noise all night, will they?" said Kate's mother, trying to keep a smile on her face. "The neighbours ..."

"They'll go quiet when it's dark," said her father. "And with a bit of luck we can get them back early in the day."

The only reason Kate agreed to go to bed at all that night was because there was nothing worth watching down at the farm. The police had set up a barrier so far back that all anyone could see were the trucks and vans and then, beyond them, inside the mesh fence, figures crouching about. It was very boring, and when P.C. Frazer told Kate it could take four hours just to get the fuse out, and that that was only the beginning, she decided to admit that she was tired.

A mixture of hens and excitement woke her up very early indeed, though. The panda on the wall-clock was pointing his bamboo shoots to five o'clock. Kate got up and dressed quietly, knowing that her parents didn't really enjoy her company this early.

Then she heard voices and stuck her head out of her bedroom door. Her father was at the bottom of the stairs, dressed, standing near the front door. "We were going to let you sleep in," he said. "We thought you'd still be tired."

"Not me," said Kate, jumping down the stairs.

"I'm going along to have a look," said her father. "Want to come?"

Kate reached the front door and hopped from foot to foot, waiting for him to open it. Some questions don't need an answer.

Even before they got to the police barriers they could see smoke coming from the direction of the duck and goose pen.

"What is it?" said Kate.

"I'm not sure," said her father.

There weren't many people at the barrier, but Mike and Jenny were there, looking as if they'd been up all night. P.C. Frazer was there, too, and so was a different Army Officer, talking to three reporters.

"What . . .?" began Kate's father. But before he could ask what the smoke was, there was a loud bang from the farmyard that made everyone jump.

"Oh," said Kate. "Oh, oh, oh."

The Army Officer heard her and raised his voice to speak to all of them. "All done, now," he said. "They've drained off the explosive and burnt it and that was them blowing up the fuse and the booster. Nice, efficient, controlled explosion. All they have to do now is clear up." He smiled at Kate. "Nothing to worry about," he said, "it often ends with a bang."

"So they haven't demolished our farm?" said Mike, laughing as though he hadn't been worried, but scratching his beard at the same time.

"Not at all," said the officer. "Just made you a bigger duck pond than you planned, that's all. Back in a minute." And he strode off towards the scene of action.

Jenny looked at Mike. "Perhaps it's meant," she said. "Shall we go for it?"

"Seems like it's done already," said Mike.

"We'll still have to neaten it up and put in a lining," said Jenny. "We'll need labourers."

Mike looked at Kate's father. "Got any spare time?" he said. "Forget the sunken bath, it seems our unexploded bomb's going to give us a real duck pond."

"An unexpected pond!" said Kate.

"Exactly that," said Jenny. "And now let's see how quickly we can get all the animals back home."

5 Who Dares Swims

"The goats think they've got police records," said Kate. "That's why they're all hyped up."

In fact it didn't take the goats long to settle down after the evacuation, but it was two days before Abigail recovered her composure, and two weeks before the hens would lay again. Every time anyone came near the sheep they bunched up together, ran a couple of yards, and then stood in a tight group, looking back over their shoulders with long, gloomy faces. Gander spent most of his time walking jerkily about with his neck stretched warningly in front of him.

"They'll all be OK soon," said Jenny. "Though Gander may take a bit longer than the others. He does so hate change."

The little fence still divided the duck and goose pen, and now it went right across the middle of the pond. "I won't shift that till Gander's got his cool back," said George.

"Polka's all right," said Alison, looking pleased with herself. "Dot and I kept her calm."

Only the ducks seemed unchanged by their experience. The Aylesburys were delighted with their new pond, and got in at once, while the other pair watched from a cautious distance, much as before.

"I know now why the Indian Runners are having a problem," said Jenny. "They were brought up at Chapel Street so they've never seen water before except in a bucket. The Aylesburys started life somewhere else, where there was a small lake, so their mother will have taught them how to swim."

The Saturday after the pond was finished, some people from Chapel Street called by to see it and Captain Welsh came, too, by special invitation. He was very impressed. "That's the most elegant bomb crater I've ever seen," he said. "You've even made a little wall round it."

"That's to stop the ducks scuffing mud into it,"
said Mike. "They like to make a muddy wallow near
water. Given a bit of time, they could fill the whole
thing in again."

Dan and Seth spotted the tall boy from Chapel
Street, and closed in, one on each side of him.

"You haven't got a pond at your farm," said Seth.

"Your ducks don't even know how to swim," said
Dan.

The boy from Chapel Street just shrugged. "I
guess we'll make one," he said. "We've got
everything else. We've probably got a bomb, too,
they'll have dropped them all along the railway." He
walked off, looking unimpressed, but Dan and Seth
punched each other in delight.

"You're jealous!" Seth yelled after him. "You're mean-eyed, green-eyed jealous, that's what you are!"

Kate, who thought Captain Welsh deserved a treat, led him off to meet Cleopatra. She wanted him to come in to the pen with her, but he stood outside it, smiling, and saying he wasn't quite sure about goats. So Kate led Cleopatra right up to the fence, where the Captain could easily reach to stroke her silky ears. However, he kept his hands behind his back.

"I haven't had much to do with animals," he said. "I really prefer to admire them from a distance."

Dan and Seth wandered up and he looked pleased to see them. "Did you want to ask anything else about the UXB?" he said hopefully. But before they could speak, he turned back to Kate. "I do see she's a very fine animal," he said. "Really. In fact she's very like my Aunt Felicity. It's just that — with animals — I never know quite what they might do."

Dan stared at him. "But you never know what a UXB might do," he said.

"I know exactly what it might do," said Captain Welsh. "And I know just how to stop it doing it. Quite different."

He didn't mind naming the ducks, though, when Jenny asked him to. He suggested Don and Dora for the Aylesburys, and Delhi and Madras for the Indian Runners.

"Delhi and Madras Dimthin," said Kate.

"Very sophisticated," said George. "None of the rest have surnames."

"Look at them," said Seth. "They're right on the edge."

"Which is which?" said Dan, as one of the pair stepped cautiously onto the small raft George had fixed at the pond's edge. "Is that Delhi?"

"Why not?" said Jenny.

The surface of the raft was about three inches under the water. Delhi stared down at his wet feet for a thoughtful moment, and then stepped off the raft. He gave a brief anxious flurry with his wings, and then his body sank down and he was swimming. Madras, horrified at being left behind, followed him.

Kate clapped and several other people joined in. "They look quite normal when they're not standing up," she said.

"Thank goodness," said Mike, beaming through his beard. "Now I can stop worrying about them. Delhi and Madras are launched."

"Who dares swims," said Dan.

"Somehow, though," Kate's father whispered in her ear, "I think they'll always be known as the Dim Thin Ducks."